DARK TIDE

DARK TIDE

SEAN RODMAN

ORCA BOOK PUBLISHERS

Published in Canada and the United States in 2023 by Orca Book Publishers.
orcabook.com

Library and Archives Canada Cataloguing in Publication
Title: Dark tide / Sean Rodman.
Names: Rodman, Sean, 1972- author.
Series: Orca anchor.
Description: Series statement: Orca anchor
Identifiers: Canadiana (print) 2022047835x | Canadiana (ebook) 20220478376 |
ISBN 9781459837119 (softcover) | ISBN 9781459837126 (PDF) |
ISBN 9781459837133 (EPUB)
Subjects: LCGFT: Novels.
Classification: LCC PS8635.O355 D37 2023 | DDC jC813/.6—dc23

Library of Congress Control Number: 2022950241

Summary: In this high-interest accessible novel for teen readers, Kai and
his stepfather must stop an ancient predator before the tide turns.

Orca Book Publishers is committed to reducing the consumption of
nonrenewable resources in the production of our books. We make
every effort to use materials that support a sustainable future.

Orca Book Publishers gratefully acknowledges the support for its publishing
programs provided by the following agencies: the Government of Canada,
the Canada Council for the Arts and the Province of British Columbia
through the BC Arts Council and the Book Publishing Tax Credit.

Design by Ella Collier
Edited by Doeun Rivendell
Cover artwork by Getty Images/Tairy and Getty Images/sergio34
Author photograph by BK Studio Photography

Printed and bound in Canada.

26 25 24 23 • 1 2 3 4

To Jasmine and Isaac,

for helping bring this monster to life.

Chapter One

The seaplane growls through the evening
sky. It skims beneath a ceiling of gray clouds.
Through the round window beside me, I
look down to the rocky coastline below.
Angry surf crashes against jagged cliffs.
Shadowy forests climb away from the edge
of the ocean.

It feels like I am trapped between the ocean below and the storm clouds above.

The seaplane is small. Behind me, the cargo hold is stuffed with supplies. Everything a scientist might need for two weeks of research.

"Dr. Ortiz, we'll need to be fast unloading your gear," says the pilot. We all wear headsets to hear each other over the roar of the engines.

"We'll be quick. There's three of us, after all," Rick says.

The pilot nods back toward me and asks, "Is this one of your students?"

Before Rick can answer, I say firmly, "No."

It's the first thing I've said this entire flight.

"Kai is my son," says Rick.

"That's not really true either," I say.

I see the pilot look over at Rick, puzzled.

Rick sighs. "He's my stepson. I got married a few months ago. It's pretty new for both of us."

"Huh," says the pilot. "So he's helping you out?"

"Sort of," says Rick. "I'm doing a research study in Blind Bay. But his mother thought that we could—"

The plane hits a pocket of turbulence and cuts him off.

Spend some time together. I finish his words in my head. My mother thought that two weeks together would make us like each other. Become a real family. I might even help with his research. Maybe get interested in school again.

Not a chance. Rick is a self-absorbed jerk. He doesn't deserve my mom.

Still, my mom needed me to try, she said. So I went along with her plan. I'll do my time out here.

But I don't like it.

We come out of the rough air. The seaplane angles away from the ocean. Begins to descend. We're flying along a narrow strip of water. This must be Blind Bay. Sharp cliffs rise on either side of us. We drop closer and closer to the rippled surface of the water. Finally the whole seaplane shudders as it touches down. The pilot guides the plane over to our temporary home.

It's basically a giant wooden raft with a small building on one end. Before we left,

Rick told me about this place. It's a mobile lab. The first floor of the building is the storage area. It has all the diving and science gear. The second floor is where scientists sleep and eat.

Outside the station there's a small inflatable boat called a Zodiac. A little floating bridge leads from the raft to the land. And, beyond that bridge, a wall of forest. This is our home for the next couple of weeks. A shack floating in the wilderness.

Literally in the middle of nowhere.

Chapter Two

I keep away from the edge of the dock. I watch the black water flex like a muscle. Pushing the big raft up and down. I hate the water. Never learned to swim. Rick taps me on the shoulder, and I turn around. He's holding out a bright-orange life jacket.

"Put this on and give us a hand, okay?"

"I don't need that," I snap. "I'm not a little kid."

"Fine. I promised your mom, but maybe we can let it go," says Rick. "Can you help, though? The pilot needs to get out of here." He walks back toward the open hatch of the plane.

"Yeah, yeah. In a second." I pull out my phone. Not even one bar of reception. *You've got to be kidding me.* I hold up the phone and swivel slowly. Still no signal. *Dammit.* I even bought a waterproof case for the phone. It's my one link to home.

"What's the Wi-Fi password here?" I yell over to him.

"Seriously, Kai? Give us a hand."

I stuff the phone back in my jacket pocket and return to the plane. The pilot is inside, handing things out. He grunts as he lifts a heavy silver canister.

"Watch that," says the pilot. "It's a scuba tank. For diving."

I take it from him. The metal surface is a little wet and hard to hold. As I turn away, it slips from my fingers and slams to the dock. There's a ringing noise that echoes over the bay.

"Kai!" yells Rick. "You've got be careful with those!"

I reach down to pick it up, but Rick waves me off. He kneels down to inspect the tank.

"You're lucky it's not damaged," he says.

"I've seen them go off like a rocket if you break the valve."

"It wasn't my fault," I mumble. "The tank was really slippery."

"Here, why don't you take this instead?" says the pilot. Grunting, he lifts out a plastic dog kennel.

There was one thing I insisted on when I agreed to this stupid plan. My dog, Alfie, needed to come with us. I needed a friend out here.

I gently place the kennel on the dock and open the metal grate. A small golden dog bounds out. Alfie rushes around the dock in circles. He runs across Rick's path. Rick stumbles and almost drops the scuba tank.

"Put his leash on him, Kai!" says Rick over his shoulder.

"Alfie just needs a run. He didn't like being trapped in the plane."

The pilot shakes his head. "Kid, be really careful when you take him onshore. This is cougar territory. And I'd say that dog has all the survival skills of a potato chip. City dogs don't always do well here."

"Right? That's what I told his mother," says Rick. "It's not safe for him here. He doesn't belong."

"You talking about Alfie or me?" I say loudly.

Rick's face tightens up. His eyes get even darker than normal.

"You know that's not what I meant."

"Whatever." I ignore Rick and scratch Alfie behind the ears.

"Kai, I have been really patient with you." Rick takes a step toward me.

"*You've* been patient? What do *you* have to deal with? I've basically been kidnapped," I say.

"What are you talking about? This was all your mom's idea!"

"Don't blame her! And what, you didn't want me to come?"

We're shouting at each other. Our voices echo across the bay. Just like the dropped scuba tank.

"No, Kai. I actually wanted you here. I

really did. Because I thought this trip might change you. Help you grow up a little."

"I'm seventeen! Don't talk to me like I'm a little kid!"

"Then stop acting like one! You're on the edge of being an adult. Which means you have to start thinking about people other than yourself."

I swallow. My throat feels raw from yelling.

Rick continues, but now his voice is low and steady. "Time to grow up, Kai. Either help unload the plane…or get out of my way."

We stare at each other for a moment. I can hear blood pounding in my ears.

"You want me out of your way?" I spin around and start to walk away. "I'm gone."

I hear Rick yell behind me. But I don't care. I gather speed as I run down the dock. My feet pound across the bridge that leads to the shore. Alfie barks and zooms ahead of me. Together we run into the woods.

Chapter Three

It feels good to run. My sneakers slap against the ground at a steady pace. Alfie leads, barking every once in a while. Letting me know he's there. We follow a rough path through the pines and cedars. They become tall shadows as the sun starts to set. The trail is overgrown, and branches scratch my arms. My lungs burn. My anger keeps me going.

I've been angry since my real dad left. Angry since Rick showed up. The anger is always there, but running dilutes it. Spreads it thin. Makes it easier to think.

Suddenly I burst out of the dark woods. It's a clearing, dimly lit by the setting sun. Fog clings to the ground like a cloudy pond. I look down. Everything below my waist dissolves into a white blur.

It's like the fog is eating me up, I think.

It's quiet. No wind. No birds. Then I realize there's no barking.

Why can't I hear Alfie anymore?

I hesitate, not wanting to move farther into the swirling fog. I look back into the shadowy woods. Maybe I can see the path.

Or maybe I'm lost.

I look around the clearing. Mist brushes my face with faint puffs. A breeze rises and shifts the surface of the fog. A gap appears, and I catch a glimpse of something. Something wrong.

It's black and wet, like a huge rotten tree stump. But I swear that the sides are moving. In and out. Just slightly. Like it's breathing.

I take a step closer, trying to figure out what I'm looking at.

The surface is weirdly slick and oily. Not like tree bark. More like...skin?

Then part of the rotten stump bends, turns—and stares at me. Black, dead eyes inspect me. It has a massive snout, like some twisted blend of a dog and a shark.

It exhales a cloud of vapor. Then slowly breathes in. Inhaling my scent.

A sudden gust of wind pushes a wall of fog between us. Rain starts to patter down around me. It drizzles down my forehead. I blink and wipe to clear my eyes.

Just like that, it's gone. Was it ever there?

Blood is rushing in my ears. I stand there, frozen. That can't have been real. I must be imagining things. And I need to find Alfie. But I know the truth, deep in my gut. That… thing…is coming for me.

I stumble back, slipping on the wet ground. Scrambling through the rainy woods.

I protect my head with both arms from the lashing branches. Now I'm running blind.

I hear something to my left. Crashing through the underbrush. I swerve away.

Just as quickly, I hear it moving toward me from my right. Again I blindly turn away from the sound. And keep running.

Then my stomach drops as I realize what's going on. I've watched videos of big cats chasing down their prey. Just like this. It's keeping me running. It's tiring me out until I'm easy to catch. Whatever this thing is, it knows I can't run forever.

It's playing with me. Like a cat with a mouse.

I'm being hunted.

Chapter Four

I trip on a muddy log and go down. But the ground seems to fall away from me. I'm rolling down a slope. Dead leaves and dirt rub against my face as I tumble. I grunt as I hit the bottom with a splash of cold water. Despite the pain, I scramble to my feet right away.

I'm standing in a creek, knee-high in water. Looking around, I start to panic. I'm trapped. The high sides of the ravine block me in. And I can't go upstream. The rain is hammering down, and the creek is surging. Pushing me downstream. I splash through the water. Until suddenly the entire stream disappears over a rocky edge. Somehow I've ended up at the top of a big waterfall.

I stare down through the dark rain. It's hard to see. But I can tell there's a ten-foot drop, at least. Straight into a pool of black water. Even if the fall doesn't kill me, I'll be pushed to the bottom. I have a vision of being trapped under the surface. Looking up, gulping in water. Drowning.

With trembling fingers, I pull my phone out of my jacket pocket. It's still intact in its waterproof case. I turn it on.

No signal. No way of calling for help.

I feel sick. I might actually die here. Nobody will ever know what happened to me.

Then I think of something. Someone needs to know. I hold the phone up, hit the video app and record.

"My name is Kai Lee," I whisper. "If anyone finds this, I'm—"

That's when I hear it. No, that's wrong—I don't hear it with my ears. I feel it. Deep inside my skull. A note so low that it vibrates right through me. Frantic, I look around. There's a shadowy outline upstream. In the dim light I can't make out much. Except that it's massive. As big as some of the old fallen trees around here. Crouched low to the ground. Staring at me, just like before.

Black eyes that don't blink. A shark's stare.

It raises its head and lets out a second roar. It's like an upside-down wolf call. Moist, low notes instead of a high, clear howl.

Then, from somewhere below, I hear something more familiar. Yipping and barking. Alfie. Down at the base of the waterfall.

The creature starts crashing through the creek toward me. Dark water splashes into the air. I face the edge of the waterfall.

No way back. No way forward.

I close my eyes. Take one step into thin air.

My mouth opens, but no sound comes out. I fall through the mist.

The hurt of the final impact is doubled by the cold. The current pushes me back to the surface like a cork. I gasp for air, clawing at the water. I need something to help me get out. But everything on the shore is slippery. I start to go under again.

Then my hand latches on to something. A slimy tree root. It's enough. Coughing, I drag myself out of the water.

I'm so tired. All I can do is lie here on my back, staring at the sky. I realize that the storm has passed, just as fast as it came. Only a few thin clouds are left. Speeding past the full moon.

I shiver against the muddy bank. I've got to move. That thing will find me. It's only a matter of time. But I can't keep running.

Turning my head, I realize there's one place I might be able to hide. I scramble to my feet. Push through the hammering sheets of water. *Through* the waterfall.

There's a little cave back here. Something small and wet rushes toward me. I nearly scream. Just in time, I realize that it's Alfie. Of course he found a hiding place. Smart dog. I scoop him into my arms and hush him quietly. Praying he won't make noise. Won't attract the creature.

We wait, hidden behind the falling water. The full moon makes the water seem to glow from the other side.

A shadow crosses between the moon and the water. Then grows larger as the creature approaches.

Alfie whimpers. I gently wrap my hand around his muzzle.

In a flash, the waterfall is pulled apart. Like a curtain being opened. Something slimy pushes through. A huge, monstrous head. Slick black skin. Tiny bead-like eyes.

A predator's eyes.

Water splashes down all around it. The massive head swings slowly. Back and forth.

Searching.

I huddle against the smooth rock wall. Trying to make myself as small as possible. I curl tighter around Alfie.

The thing's lips shrink back in a snarl,

revealing rows of pointy teeth. Frustrated.
Or hungry.

Then it swings away from us. Like we
weren't there at all. Its head turns slightly to
one side. Like a cat listening for its prey.

But I realize that the thundering water
protects us. The thing can't hear us. Or smell
us. Or even see us huddled at the back of
this dark cave.

With a sudden jerk, the monster's head
pulls back through the curtain of water.

There's a deep roar from the other side of
the waterfall.

Then nothing.

Alfie and I wait. Maybe it's just minutes,
but it feels like hours. We wait to hear the
creature again. Afraid it might come back.

Soon I can't handle the cold anymore. I carefully push my way back through the waterfall. The moon is bright, showing me that we're alone. My eyes darting left and right, I creep back into the woods. Alfie senses the danger too. He slinks beside me quietly.

We're the prey. Our only defense is silence.

Chapter Five

"Kai!"

Somewhere out there, Rick is calling my name. A few minutes later I can see his flashlight in the distance. It's like a lighthouse beam, sweeping back and forth. Guiding me home. I run toward it. Branches slap against my face. Finally Alfie and I burst into the clearing where Rick is standing. Surprised, he shines the light right at us.

"Kai! Where the hell have you been?" Rick says. "You were gone for hours!"

I lift an arm to shield my eyes.

"There's something out there," I gasp, still panting from the run. "Something weird."

Rick keeps talking like he didn't hear me.

"You can't just take off like that! This is a dangerous place. You should have come straight back. You don't understand—"

"It's not my fault!" I shout. Then I cringe. It might still be out there. Listening for us. I drop my voice to a whisper. "I was trapped. There's a…thing…out there. It chased me. A monster."

That stops him.

"A monster," Rick says. "Like, a grizzly? Cougar?"

"No," I say. I kneel down and wrap my arms around Alfie. His fur is still damp. "Like, a full-on monster. Something out of a movie. It chased me. I had to hide from it. Behind this waterfall. And I found Alfie there. Then we escaped."

"A monster chased you behind a waterfall," says Rick calmly. "And that's why you didn't come back."

"I know it sounds crazy."

"Actually, yeah," says Rick. "It really does. Look, let's get you back—"

I'm tired and wet and just want to feel safe. But more than that, I suddenly want Rick to believe me. Maybe just so I don't feel crazy.

"Wait—I have proof!" I pull out my phone. Hopefully the waterproof case has protected it. I find the video I took earlier and press *play*. My voice whispers out of the speaker.

"My name is Kai Lee. If anyone finds this, I'm—"

Then there's that sound. The weird call the monster made.

An unearthly sound.

"Okay," says Rick after a moment. "But that could be a bear. Or raccoon."

I stare at him. "For sure it was not a raccoon. This thing was huge. With teeth. And a lizard tail."

"What, like a...dragon? Kai. listen to me. Listen. Something really could have killed you tonight. Like exposure or hypothermia.

Because you were reckless." He crosses his arms.

"Stop trying to blame me for this! There's something out there!" I point back toward the darkness. Toward the woods and the waterfall.

"I don't want to hear about it," says Rick firmly.

"Then what do you want to hear?"

"I want to hear you say that you're sorry!" says Rick.

"For what?" I yell. My voice sounds way too loud, and I look over my shoulder. Rick must see how scared I am, because he softens his voice.

"For not listening to me. For making me worry. I was terrified that I'd lost you! Do you have any idea how worried I was?"

"Right. You were just worried about what my mom would think if I got hurt."

But the words sound immature, even to me.

Rick takes a deep breath. "Kai, you risked your own life. Just because you were so angry at me. But I'm your parent, whether you like it or not. And that means I'm here for you, no matter what. You just scared me tonight. And that turned into anger."

In the dim glow from the flashlight, I can see his face. He's focused intently on me. But the eyes behind the glasses are kind. A little scared.

"I just found this family, with you and your mom. I don't want to lose you," he continues. "I guess that's why I want you to apologize.

I want us to trust each other. Because that's what families do, right?"

I let go of Alfie and stand up, wobbling a little.

"I guess so," I say. "But I'm not lying to you. There's something out there. You need to trust me on that."

Rick stares at me for a long moment. Then he just turns toward the research station. His flashlight leads the way through the dark forest. It's silent except for the crunching of the dry leaves underfoot.

I keep looking over my shoulder into the darkness.

Chapter Six

The windows of the research station glow like stars against the black night. Rick heads straight inside. The bottom floor is kind of like a garage. But filled with diving gear and science equipment. Alfie and I follow Rick up a set of stairs to the second floor. He goes right over to a small stove and starts cooking. Meanwhile, Alfie and I wander around.

There's not much to explore. Two air mattresses and sleeping bags. One small bathroom. A table covered with laptops and electronics. More scuba tanks and wet suits crammed in a corner.

Pretty soon Rick pushes some of the gear on the table to one side. He puts down two bowls of steaming soup. Alfie gets a bowl of dog food on the floor.

Rick and I eat in silence.

After a while Rick pushes away his bowl. "Your little adventure put me behind schedule," he says. "I've got to finish some work. You can get ready for bed."

Rick leans over and drags a laptop in front of us. He taps some keys, and an image appears on the screen. It's a grainy, blue-green video. Like a view from a spaceship slowly flying through some weird alien tunnel.

There's a noise every few seconds. A rush of static, like a wave. I want to pretend I'm not interested, just to bug him. I pretend to yawn, which turns into a real one. Finally I have to ask.

"What is that? It looks like a really boring video game."

Despite himself, Rick laughs a little.

"This was the view from Rover 1. It was one of my underwater robots. They use sound waves to map caves at the bottom of Blind Bay. They usually run on their own, twenty-four hours a day. Exploring the caves."

"Usually?" I ask.

"The last time I was here, I left Rover 1 running. It was fine. And then it just stopped sending back data to the university. That's why I'm back. To send a new robot into the caves."

"What happened to Rover 1?"

Rick shrugs. "I don't know. That's what I'm watching. The last data that Rover 1 sent us."

We watch for a while. The image doesn't change much. The underwater cave slowly moves past as Rover 1 explores it. There's the rush of static again from the speakers. Another sound pulse.

Suddenly the footage gets darker, then shakes wildly. Like the camera collided with something. Then the screen goes black. Rick rewinds the footage.

"Could be a gas bubble," Rick mutters. "I wish I knew what went wrong."

He gets up from the table and returns with a silver plastic case. He clicks it open to reveal a robot. It doesn't look like much. A yellow disc with six propellers on the outside. A big camera lens sits on the front.

"Anyway, this is Rover 2. He'll go out tomorrow."

"It looks like a drone. I got one for my birthday last year," I say. "It flew into a tree and got shredded."

"This one is a little different. Doesn't fly. Just swims. And more expensive, for sure. Hopefully tougher."

I nod, unable to contain another yawn.

Rick laughs. "It's way past midnight. Get some sleep, kid."

I'm honestly too tired to argue. I unroll my sleeping bag on an air mattress and crawl in. Alfie tucks in beside me, and I curl my fingers in his fur. I watch Rick for a while, bent over his laptop. He looks like a ghost in the blue light from the screen. Then I'm out.

Chapter Seven

Outside, something metal clatters to the ground. I wake up with a start. I sit up fast and look over at Rick. He's still working at the table. But now he's listening, head tilted to one side.

"Go back to sleep," he says, distracted. "It's five in the morning. You've only been asleep for a few hours."

Again, a noise from the dock. Like some-thing pushing over gear.

Rick and I look at each other.

"Probably just a raccoon or something." Rick gets up and starts toward the stairs. "I'll be right back."

"Wait!" I say. "It might be—"

"What? A monster?" says Rick. He shakes his head and disappears downstairs.

After a moment, I follow him.

I quietly make my way down the stairs. Then through the cluttered storage room. Standing by the open door, I look out at the bay. The full moon is about to set. But the light casts a silver glow over the wilderness. It hits home again just how alone we are. Thousands of miles of forest between us and anyone else. As if sensing my fear, Alfie leans against my leg. I watch Rick move down the dock. He carefully steps into the small boat that's tied up there—the Zodiac.

Then, just beyond him, movement catches my eye. Something sleek and black emerges from the water. A dark bump. It shines under the moonlight for a moment. Then sinks away.

Maybe it was just a wave.

My breath starts to come in tiny little gasps.

Rick is still in the Zodiac. Head down, fiddling with something.

The black shape surfaces again. Nearer Rick and the Zodiac. Larger this time. Then vanishes.

It's circling. Like a shark.

Rick's the one being hunted this time. He's the prey.

I could slip back up the stairs. It's not like I could stop this thing, even if I wanted to. I grab Alfie by the collar and start backing up toward the stairs. Toward safety. The smart thing to do would be to escape again. Run, like last time.

But Rick said he'd be there for me, no matter what.

If I run again, Rick is dead.

I quickly step out onto the dock.

"Rick! It's here! Get out!" I yell as loudly as I can.

He climbs out of the boat onto the dock. But then he just stands there, looking at me.

"What?" he says. "I didn't hear what—"

Too late.

With a surge of water, the monster leaps out from the depths. It crashes onto one end of the dock, causing the whole structure to bounce wildly. Like a tidal wave slamming into us.

Rick stumbles around and faces the creature. His flashlight reveals the size of the thing. As tall as Rick. But as long as a big pickup truck. Four legs, slung low to the ground like an alligator. A long, flat tail slithers behind it.

And those black, unblinking eyes. Cold. Hungry.

It lunges. Rick yells, falling backward into a pile of gear. The creature misses him by inches. Boxes scatter around it.

It rears back for a second try. Rick reaches into the scattered pile. Grabs an empty metal storage bin. He holds it up like a shield. The creature lunges again.

Its teeth crunch into the metal. The bin crumples. Like a can of soda in your hand. The creature stops for a moment, shaking its head. The mangled steel is dangling from its mouth.

Rick lies there on his back. Terrified. Defenseless.

I need to give him time to escape. That means putting myself out there as bait. I take a deep breath.

Then I scream at the creature. Alfie joins in, barking wildly.

But the monster doesn't care. It drops the metal bin. Creeps closer to Rick. It's totally focused on him. And I need to shake that focus.

Then I remember something that might do it. The video I took on my phone. I pull it out and turn the volume up to max. And hit *play*.

Chapter Eight

The sound isn't loud. But the eerie noise carries through the quiet night. The call that's like a cross between a wolf and a whale.

The monster stops.

It slowly turns its head from side to side. Trying to find the source of the noise. Confused. Curious.

Rick scrambles back toward me.

"Go! Back upstairs! Go!" he hisses.

Before the creature can move, we're back in the research station. Rick pushes me inside, then slams the door shut. He jams a scuba tank against it. We all clatter back up the stairs. Rick shuts the door behind us. And I push a chair against it. That won't stop the creature. But it makes me feel better.

"I don't understand," says Rick. He takes off his glasses. With shaking hands, he polishes them with his shirt. "What was that? That wasn't like anything I've ever seen. Some kind of elephant seal? Or crocodile? That's ridiculous. What the hell is it?"

His voice is high-pitched. A little out of control.

"It's the monster," I say evenly.

54

He puts on his glasses and stares at me. "The same thing that attacked you and Alfie?"

I nod. I feel myself start to tremble. Part of me hadn't believed my own story. Couldn't explain what I had seen with my own eyes.

But I can see Rick starting to believe it as well. We're in this together now.

And suddenly it's all way too real. I squish my lips together, trying hard not to cry. But it doesn't work.

"Rick, I know I screwed up by running away," I say. "And I know you've tried to be nice to me. I am sorry for—everything."

Rick shrugs. "Kai, you don't have to explain."

"No, I do. Remember when you said before that you were scared of losing me?

And that made you angry? I think I was kind of a jerk to you because I was scared too. Scared that everything was changing. That I might lose my mom to you."

Rick looks a little shocked. Then he awkwardly puts an arm around my shoulder. But I lean into it and hug him.

"I'm not taking anything away from your family, Kai. Just adding something."

I wipe the back of my hand across my runny nose.

"Anyway, I guess we both have something else to be scared about," I say.

Rick laughs. But it's cut short by a violent slamming outside. The creature is trying to find a way in.

Then there's a noise from the laptop. Static. The video from Rover 1 has looped back. It's playing again. I look over. Wait— there's something about the image that just flashed by.

I hurry over to the table. "Can you show me the last thing Rover 1 saw before it stopped working?"

Rick pulls the laptop toward him. He keys in a command, and the video rewinds. Then it starts playing back at twice the normal speed. We lean over the screen. Rover 1 floats through the underwater cave. Craggy walls slide by, lit by the robot's lights.

Suddenly there's movement. A large

black shape shoots out from deep within the cave. Right at the camera.

"There. Just after one of the sound pulses," says Rick. He rewinds and freezes the image. It's blurry. He zooms in. "I didn't see it before."

A shark-like black eye stares at us from the screen.

"The monster—it came from the cave?" I ask.

Rick nods.

"A species we've never seen before," he says, almost whispering. "I wonder how long it's been in the cave system. Maybe it was hibernating there."

I shrug. "Like a bear?"

"Kind of. But sleeping for hundreds— thousands?—of years. That would explain why nobody has seen it before," Rick says. Now he's smiling in his sad way. "Do you realize what this means?"

I shake my head.

"This is a huge scientific discovery. We're going to be part of history. Maybe they'll even name this species after us."

We're interrupted by the sound of crunching wood outside. The windows rattle in their frames from the impact. Alfie whines and hides under the table, leaning against my legs.

We wait silently. Listening. Another slam that shakes the building.

"I think your scientific discovery wants to eat us," I whisper.

Rick looks pale. He speaks like he's thinking

things through. "The robot and the sound pulses woke this thing up. It destroyed Rover 1. It came out of the cave."

"So we just need to tell it to go back in the cave?" I ask.

Rick laughs. "Sure. Maybe if Rover 2 just asks politely?"

Something clicks in my head.

"Hang on," I say. "What if Rover 2 could lure it back somehow? It can play sounds, right? So what if it played that recording from my phone? The monster paid attention to that."

"Yeah, that's not a bad theory," Rick says. "But then there's a problem with the tide."

"The tide?" I ask. Alfie peeks out from under the table. Nuzzles against my hand.

I scratch behind his ears. "What's that got to do with it?"

"The bay has a really strong tidal current. Everything gets flushed out to the ocean. That's part of what makes it interesting for scientists. The high rate of flow means—"

There's a grinding noise outside. Something sliding along the side of the building.

"Ah, I'll save the lecture. We can't just throw Rover 2 in the bay anytime we want. It has to be timed right. So it won't get sucked out to sea by the tide," says Rick. "If it did, it could end up anywhere."

Alfie whines nervously. I gently stroke his fur, then freeze. I look up at Rick.

"The tide is going to flush everything in the bay out to sea?" I ask.

Rick nods. "Everything. Pretty much."

"Including our monster," I say.

Rick nods, more slowly this time. "Yeah. That thing could end up anywhere on the coast."

"So how long do we have?" I ask.

Rick searches through a pile of binders and papers. He pulls out a chart filled with numbers and squints at it.

"About an hour. Till sunrise."

Chapter Nine

"We can't let that happen," I say.

Rick stands up and starts shoving papers and the laptop into a backpack. He shakes his head. "This is all bigger than we can handle. You can't stop the tide, Kai. And I don't think we can stop this creature. We need to get to the Zodiac. There's a marine radio on board. I'll radio for help, and we can get out of here."

"You can't just leave. You started this," I say. "You woke it up."

"This is not my fault," Rick says sharply. We look at each other for a moment. He can see the disappointment in my face. "Okay, you're right. I sent the robot in there."

He steps toward me. Puts his hands on my shoulders. "Maybe the police or the navy can deal with this thing. But my priority is keeping you safe. That's the most important thing to me. I already lost you once tonight."

I can see in his eyes that he's scared. Not just because of the monster. But at the idea of me getting hurt.

"Okay," I say. "I get it. Let's get out of here."

Rick finishes packing the backpack. He grabs the case with Rover 2 in it. Then we gently move the chair away from the door. We creep down the stairs and into the storage room. I look through the window onto the dock.

The creature is still there. Waiting near the Zodiac. The dim light from the upstairs windows reflects off its oily black skin. Slowly it opens its massive jaw and calls out into the night. Then listens. Waiting for another creature to respond. But the night is silent.

I shiver at the sound. But it's also kind of sad. What would it be like to wake up and find that you were the last of your kind?

"I could use the recording on my phone again," I whisper.

"Too risky," says Rick. "It might just come after us. We need to get that thing to move away."

I look around the storage room. Something glints off the beam of my flashlight. The silver air canister leaning against the door.

"Remember when I dropped that scuba tank on the dock? You said they could go off like a rocket?"

Rick nods. "Yeah, if the valve is damaged. The tank wouldn't go in a straight line. But it would make a lot of noise. Definitely get the creature's attention."

He grabs a heavy wrench from a set of tools on the wall. Then he pulls the air tank away so I can open the door. Rick carefully puts the tank outside. He points the base of it toward the monster. The end facing us has a dial and valve on it.

"Stand back," says Rick. He pulls back and swings down hard. There's a ringing sound, like a bell.

The creature turns toward us.

Nothing happens. The valve isn't damaged.

"Rick," I say. "Maybe this was a bad idea."

He swings again. Harder.

Another clear ringing sound as the wrench bounces off the valve.

Again, nothing. The monster starts to slide across the dock toward us. Slowly gaining speed. Alfie barks madly and I clutch him to my chest.

Rick swings again.

This time there's no ringing sound. Instead there's a loud bang. The tank blasts forward, skidding over the damp wooden boards of the dock. It skitters in different directions. Pinging off posts and gear as it shoots toward the creature.

The monster lunges at the tank as it flashes by, then turns to chase it. The tank flies off the edge and hits the water with a splash. And the creature follows, causing a surge of water across the dock.

Then there's silence. Until both Rick and I laugh with relief.

"That was like Alfie chasing a ball!" I say.

"I can't believe your plan worked! Now get to the Zodiac!"

Chapter Ten

A few seconds later we're in the boat, pushing away from the dock. Rick keeps the speed low, trying not to attract the monster's attention. I settle Alfie in the back on some tarps. Once we're underway, Rick turns on the marine radio.

"I'll try and get through to the coast guard. It might take a little while. Can you steer?"

He gestures for me to take the wheel. "It's easy. Just keep it in a straight line."

I stand up and take over. There's static as Rick adjusts the radio.

After a moment I ask, "Rick? Where's the underwater cave?"

"About a thousand feet from here. It's in the other direction—back into the bay. We want to head toward the open ocean."

I turn the wheel, and the boat swings in a curve. Toward the cave.

"What are you doing?" yells Rick. "You're going the wrong way!"

"You said it's only about an hour until the tide turns, right?" I ask. "And then that monster will be pulled out to sea."

"What are you doing, Kai?" Rick asks again, more quietly. He studies me. The dim glow of the instrument panel is reflected on his glasses.

"Say you manage to get through to the coast guard eventually. And you get them to believe you. Even then, there's no way they'll be able to find and catch that thing. Not before the tide turns."

Rick is silent for a moment. "I made a promise to your mother, Kai. To keep you safe out here. To bring you home. We can't handle this thing on our own."

"I think we can," I say. "And I want to go home. Believe me, I really, really do. But I'm asking you to trust me. I've got a plan."

"We're here." Rick takes the controls from me, and the boat slows to a stop. "You've got one minute to explain yourself. Then I'm taking us out of here."

I take a breath and pull my thoughts together. "The creature keeps making that sound. That weird call, right? And when I played the video on my phone, you saw what happened. It's like the monster is listening for that same call."

The boat bounces in the waves. Rick nods, and I continue.

"So what if we load that recording—the call—into Rover 2? And instead of sending out the pulses of noise that woke it up, we send out the recording? The monster comes to check it out. Then we send Rover 2 deep into the cave, and the monster follows. Like Alfie chasing a ball. But we send them both *really* deep into the cave. Where the tide can't pull the monster out. We'll send it home."

"The odds of this working are pretty small," Rick says.

"At least we will have tried. Worst case? We fail, and the monster escapes the bay anyway."

"I don't think that's the very worst case," mutters Rick.

"So we'll use Rover 2 as bait?" I ask.

"Worst fishing trip ever. But yes, it might work. And you're right—we don't have time to call for help. Sun's coming up. Tide's turning."

There's a rosy glow around the mountains that surround the bay. And I can feel the tide starting to pull at our little boat. Alfie moves from his bed at the back and leans against me. He whines softly. He's worried too.

Rick puts on a headlamp and flicks it on. He sets to work with Rover 2, the laptop and my phone. After a few minutes he unplugs everything.

"Okay, let's give this a shot," Rick says. "Take the wheel again. But keep the boat really steady while I put Rover 2 in the water."

I move into position, and Rick leans over the side. The beam from his headlamp glitters on the water. A wave slaps against the boat, and Rick stumbles. He almost drops Rover 2.

He tightens his grip, then looks over at me. "Easy, Kai. Try turning the boat into the current."

Rick's eyes are focused on me. He doesn't see the dark shape rushing up from the depths. But I see it.

The black eyes.

Open jaw.

Rows and rows of white teeth.

As it breaks the surface, I let go of the wheel and shove Rick out of the monster's path. He drops Rover 2 into the water but falls safely onto the bottom of the boat.

The monster lunges into the air, like a shark in a feeding frenzy. It crashes back into the water. And a huge wave of saltwater splashes around us.

I look toward Rick, lying flat on the boat. He's not moving.

"Rick!"

As I rush toward him, the boat rocks like crazy in the waves. The floor is slick with water. My feet slide out from under me. I have a sickening falling sensation, just like at the waterfall. And the shock of cold water as I hit the water.

I'm overboard.

Chapter Eleven

I feel myself being pulled down by my heavy clothes. Looking up, I can see the surface. The glow of the sunrise above the water.

Looking down, nothing but darkness.

Something whirs past me. I panic, thinking it's the monster. But it's not. Rover 2 must have started up when it landed in the water. The little robot heads into the deep. Fast and steady. Then I hear it play my recording of the monster's call. The upside-down wolf call. The video I took just last night. Less than ten hours earlier. It feels like a million years ago.

The sound fades as Rover 2 disappears into the dark.

I'm headed down too.

I start to struggle, flailing my arms. I hate the water. Never learned to swim. The more I struggle, the weaker I get. Until I can't move anymore.

Floating in the cold emptiness, a weird peace comes over me. I did the right thing. I tried to fix our mistakes. I tried to save Rick. I didn't run away.

Then I hear the call again. But so much louder. Underwater, the sound feels like it is all around me. In my bones. The low, sad call of the monster.

Then again. But farther away. Deeper.

It must be working. The creature must be following Rover 2. And into the cave. I smile, then release the last of my breath into the water. The bubbles tickle my face as they float upward.

One more time I hear the call. It's almost gone, down into the deep.

And I'm almost gone too.

Light fills my entire world. I blink but can't see beyond the bright glare.

Then I throw up. Salty seawater hurls out of me.

"Thought I lost you again," says Rick, panting. He's soaking wet, kneeling next to me on the floor of the Zodiac. "I kept diving and diving for you. Didn't think I could. Finding you was a miracle."

I throw up again.

"Miracles shouldn't feel this awful," I mumble.

Rick laughs. He turns off the headlamp that was blinding me. Alfie nuzzles against me, trying to make me feel better. Rick wraps me up in a blanket.

The Zodiac is drifting, waves slapping against the rubber hull. The orange light of sunrise reflects off the calm water of the bay. It's like nothing ever happened.

"Did it work?" I ask, leaning against the side of the boat. "Is it gone?"

"See for yourself," says Rick. He sits beside me and pulls out the laptop. There's the video feed from Rover 2. It shows the tunnel walls sliding past. The robot is speeding deeper and deeper into the cave.

"It's at almost two thousand feet. It's never gone this deep. I'll lose contact soon."

A black shape appears on the edge of the screen, then drops behind the camera. It's the creature. Swimming with Rover 2. Following the sound.

There's a flash of static. Then the words *No Signal* appear.

"That's it," says Rick. "It's out of range.

But Rover 2 will keep going until the batteries give out. Or the pressure crushes it. Either way, the two of them will be far away from the surface. There's no way the tide can get them now."

We sit in silence for a moment. The sun rises. Colors appear around us. The rich green of the pines. Sparkling light off the deep blue water of the bay. White foam as the waves surge against the rocks.

It's the same view as when I arrived. But now it seems different. Safe. More like home.

"So are you going to name your huge scientific discovery?" I ask Rick. "You're going to be so famous."

"Well, maybe I'll name it after you," says Rick. "You can be kind of a monster yourself."

I reach over and weakly punch him on the shoulder. "Fair."

"But seriously, I'm not going to name it. In fact, I don't think I'll tell anyone about it." Rick rubs a hand through his dark hair. "I think some things are better left...undiscovered."

I nod. "So it's our secret?"

"For now, yeah. I'll have to keep an eye on it."

"But you'll need a research assistant, right? To keep studying those caves? Someone who knows the truth?"

Rick looks over at me. He looks tired. But happy.

"Definitely," he says. "Want a job next summer?"

MORE CAN'T-PUT-THEM-DOWN READS BY SEAN RODMAN

A strange exchange student with wild stories about mobsters and hackers offers to pay Ryan to be his bodyguard. Easy money, right?

"Readers will be enticed by the edgy theme and compelling story."
—*School Library Journal*

Josh discovers a virtual town that is eerily similar to his own.

"A gripping read."
—*Resource Links*

SEAN RODMAN

NIGHT TERRORS

Dylan struggles with the memories of the death of his younger brother while fighting for survival in a snowbound resort.

"Fast-paced and intense."
—*School Library Journal*

Michael's grandfather, a retired cat burglar, helps him steal back a valuable necklace.

"Full of suspense."
—*CM Reviews*

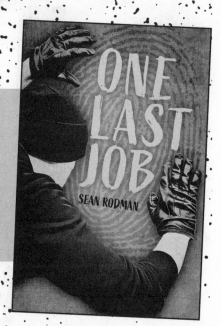

ONE LAST JOB

SEAN RODMAN

STAR EATERS
BROOKE CARTER

IN A FAR-OFF
GALAXY, ENTIRE
WORLDS
ARE DYING.

WHAT SEEMS LIKE
A DREAM COME
TRUE QUICKLY
TURNS INTO A
NIGHTMARE.

TRAPPED
SIGMUND BROUWER

Sean Rodman is the author of numerous books for young people, including *One Last Job* in the Orca Anchor line and *The Bodyguard* and *Firewall* in the Orca Soundings line. Sean is the executive director of Story Studio, a charity that inspires, educates and empowers youth to be great storytellers. He lives in Victoria, British Columbia.

For more information on all the books

in the Orca Anchor line, please visit

orcabook.com